Fic
Fri   Friedman, Carl
        Nightfather

Nightfather

Nightfather

Carl Friedman

Translated from the Dutch by
Arnold and Erica Pomerans

PERSEA BOOKS  NEW YORK

Originally published under the title *Tralievader* in 1991 by Uitgeverij G. A. van Oorschot, Amsterdam. First published in the United States of America in 1994 by Persea Books, New York.

Portions of *Nightfather* have been previously published in *Icarus 14*.

For information, write to the publisher:
Persea Books, Inc.
60 Madison Avenue
New York, New York 10010

This publication has been made possible in part by the financial support of the Dutch Literary Foundation.

Library of Congress Cataloging-in-Publication Data
Friedman, Carl.
[Tralievader. English]
Nightfather : a novel / Carl Friedman ; translated from the Dutch by Arnold and Erica Pomerans.
p. cm.
ISBN 0-89255-193-3
1. Holocaust survivors—Netherlands—Fiction. I. Pomerans, Arnold. II. Pomerans, Erica. III. Title.
PT5881.16.R48T7313   1994
839.3'1364—dc20   94-15596   CIP

Designed by REM Studio, Inc.
Set in Abadi Light by ComCom, Allentown, Pennsylvania.
Printed and bound by The Haddon Craftsmen, Scranton, Pennsylvania.
Jacket photograph: *Terezin, 1992* by Leo Divendal,
copyright © 1992 by Leo Divendal.
Reproduced by permission of the photographer.

First Edition

For my son Aron

Nightfather

Camp

He never mentions it by name. It might have been Trebibor or Majdawitz, Soblinka or Birkenhausen. He talks about "the camp," as if there had been just one.

"After the war," he says, "I saw a film about the camp. With prisoners frying an egg for breakfast." He slaps his forehead with the palm of his hand. "An egg!" he says shrilly. "In the camp!"

So camp is somewhere where no one fries eggs.

Camp is not so much a place as a condition. "I've had camp," he says. That makes him different from us. We've had chicken pox and German measles. And after Simon fell out of a tree, he got a concussion and had to stay in bed for weeks.

But we've never had camp.

Most of the time he drops the past participle for convenience. Then he says "I have camp," as if the situation hadn't changed. And it's true, it hasn't. He still has camp, especially in his face. Not so much in his nose or his ears, although they're big enough, but in his eyes.

I saw a wolf in the zoo once, with eyes like that. He was pacing back and forth in his cage, up and down and up and down, to the front and back again. I spent a long time staring at him through the bars.

Full of worry, I went to look for Max and Simon. They were hanging over the railings around the monkey rock, laughing at a baboon throwing pebbles.

"Please, come and look at the wolf," I said, but they weren't interested. Only when I started to cry did Max reluctantly turn away and follow me.

"Well?" he said in a bored voice when we were standing in front of the wolf's cage. "What's the matter with him?"

"He has camp!" I sobbed. Max glanced through the bars.

"Impossible," he said. "Wolves don't get camp."

Then he pulled me by the hand. I had to go back to the monkeys with him.

When we got home and my mother saw my tear-stained cheeks, she asked what had made me unhappy. Max shrugged.

"She isn't big enough yet for the zoo."

Nice

Max is drinking from a puddle. He's lying flat in the mud, sucking the brown water up through a straw.

"What does it taste like?" we ask impatiently. But he shuts his eyes contemptuously and goes on sucking.

"You little pig!" my mother calls from afar. "You'll make yourself sick!"

We have to go inside, even Simon and I, although we haven't had our turn at tasting yet.

During the night, Max complains about feeling sick. He clutches his stomach and groans, "I must have swallowed worms. I can feel them wriggling!"

You don't get camp from drinking muddy water. You don't get camp from playing outside without your coat on or from never washing your hands. I don't know how or why my father got camp. Maybe he got it because he's different from most of the people I know. Because he's different, my mother is different, too. And because the two of them are different, Max, Simon, and I are different from ordinary children. At home you don't notice it, but at school you do.

"A man flying through the air!" The teacher smiles as she bends over my drawing.

"He isn't flying," I tell her, "he's hanging. See, he's dead, his tongue is blue. And these prisoners have to look at him as a punishment. My father is there, too. Here, he's the one with the big ears."

"That's nice," says the teacher.

"It's not," I say. "They're starving and now they have to wait a long time for their soup." But she's already moved on to the next desk.

"Two pixies on a toadstool," she calls out, clapping her hands. "That's really nice!"

In a rage I make great scrawls across my drawing and turn the paper over. What's so nice about a couple of pixies? I draw a whole lot more than two: five in the snow and one on top of the watchtower.

Roll Call

He doesn't have camp only in his face but in his fingers, too. They often drum nervously on the edge of the table or on the arms of his chair.

And he has camp in his feet. In the middle of the night his feet slide out of bed, carrying him down the stairs and through the hallway. We can hear him far away, opening and closing doors without ever finding the peace he's looking for behind any of them.

"Were you on the prowl again last night?" my mother asks when we are at breakfast. He nods. She puts her hand over his. "Ephraim," she says, "Ephraim."

Sometimes his prowling wakes us up. Then we go downstairs in our pajamas to keep him company. He walks around in circles while we watch him from the sofa. When my mother comes in, he stops.

"I'm keeping you all up," he mumbles. She rubs her eyes and sighs.

"Never mind," she says. "You're alive, that's what counts. You can dance on the roof all night as far as I'm concerned."

He bends over her. She nudges her forehead into the hollow at the bridge of his nose. Their faces fit together like a jigsaw puzzle.

One night Simon and I are woken up by loud thumps. Together we go to see what's happening. The landing light is on. We stand on the cold linoleum, blinking in its glare. The door to the main bedroom is open. My father is lying on the floor inside. His eyebrow is bleeding. Max and my mother are kneeling beside him.

"You take his other arm," my mother says, "otherwise he'll fall against the closet again."

They pull him to his feet. As soon as he's up, he jumps to attention and brings his hand to his head.

"Caps off," he whispers in German. He lets his arm drop to his side, then jerks it up again. "Caps on." There's blood on his fingers.

Roll Call

"No, Ephraim." My mother takes him by the shoulders. Max skips around the two of them like a puppy.

"The bell for roll call has rung," says my father in a voice I don't recognize.

"There isn't any bell here," my mother says, pushing him toward the bed. "You're home, with me."

When he's sitting on the edge of the bed, she turns around without letting him go and says, "It's all right, go back to bed now."

Deep down under the covers I start to cry.

"Don't be frightened," says Simon. "It isn't real. Papa's been dreaming everything, the bell and the roll call."

"And the blood?" I ask him from under the blankets. "Did he dream that, too?"

There is no reply.

Bon Appetit

"That's your third helping," my mother says to Max. "Make sure you leave room for the cherries." He nods.

"I could easily eat a whole pound of cherries, I'm so hungry."

"You, hungry?" My father laughs. "You don't even know the meaning of the word."

"Yes, I do," says Max indignantly. "It's when your stomach growls."

My father shakes his head.

"When you're really hungry, it doesn't growl, it gnaws. You're completely empty inside and as limp as a punctured balloon." His eyes grow distant. "You can't even begin to understand," he says. "We had to work for twelve hours a day or more, and all we got to eat was beetroot soup and a lump of bread. The beetroot soup was a sort of cloudy water which had never even seen a beetroot. Now and then something would float up to the top, but no one had any idea what it was.

"The soup was doled out by Sigismund the Flogger. Sigi was a Pole and much stronger than we were. He never lost a single ounce of weight in the camp. Every day he held back some of our soup and then swapped it for cigarettes. With the cigarettes he bought bread, goulash, blankets. He even had wool underwear.

"There was an enormous steel ladle hanging from his belt which he used for pouring the soup into our bowls. If anyone new dared to complain about the quality of the soup, he got his brains bashed in with that ladle. Then Sigi would point to the mess and say, 'Be grateful! Now you can have meat in your soup, too!' "

"And how much bread did you get?" Simon asks.

My father holds out his hand over the plates and the empty bowls and pinches the air. There's a narrow space between his forefinger and his thumb.

"That much," he says, "and even less later on. It was made out of flour mixed with straw and sawdust."

"Sawdust?" Simon makes a face. "Like Jonah's?"

Jonah is our hamster. Every week Max sprinkles fresh sawdust over the bottom of his cage.

"You don't understand," my father says.

He gets up, but the bread ration continues to hover over the table like a ghost. I look at it helplessly and feel a sudden disgust for the cherries my mother is serving.

How very lucky we are.

The SS

My mother is busy sticking a piece of cardboard up over the sink. She has written BRUSH YOUR TEETH! on it in big red letters. I'm especially impressed by the exclamation mark.

"That's the way to tell the children," says my father in a mocking voice. He's standing in the doorway to the bathroom, his hands in his pockets.

"Decent shoes and good teeth are the pillars of society," my mother says.

"Maybe so, but do you really have to put up signs on the wall?"

"If I feel like it," says my mother defensively.

"Maybe you'll feel like putting up a few more tomorrow, in German, with, say, 'Bath and Disinfection' or 'It Is
Your Duty to Keep Clean!' "

"Don't be like that," says my mother. She pulls the
cardboard off the wall and walks away.

"Well?" he says, turning to me. "Shouldn't you be
brushing your teeth? *Schnell!*" He laughs.

"It was a good sign," I say gravely, squeezing toothpaste onto my brush. By way of belated homage to the sign,
I give all my teeth an extra good brushing.

When I've rinsed my mouth, I turn to see my father
pacing up and down on the landing. "When the SS felt
bored," he says, "they'd pick a prisoner at random, take off
his cap, and fling it up high onto the barbed wire. 'Go fetch
your cap,' they'd shout, 'or you'll get a bullet in the back!' "

I nod. Barefooted, I go to the bedroom. Simon is
staying at a friend's. His bed is scarily empty. Max is allowed
to stay up late because he's the oldest. The moment I'm
under the blankets, my father's head appears around the
door.

"But the barbed wire was electrified," he says. "It
takes the SS to dream up something like that."

Though my mother has tucked me in, I can't fall asleep. I go
and sit on Simon's bed, by the window. Gently I push the
curtains apart. It's windy outside. Clouds with dragons'

backs are chasing one another across the sky. Max says that space is infinite and that there are too many stars to count. Even if you spent your entire life counting them, not eating or sleeping or going to the bathroom, you still wouldn't ever reach the end.

I sit on Simon's bed and look at the sky. The black is blacker than usual. I'm almost sucked up into it. Max says that when it's night here, it's daytime somewhere else in the world. But what's the use of that? It takes the SS to dream up a thing like that. And the bit about the stars, too.

Up, Up, and Away

It's Saturday. We're having breakfast. My father never actually eats in the morning, but he's still very busy. He drinks coffee, smokes cigarettes, and tells stories. We listen. That suits us, because my mother doesn't allow us to talk with our mouths full anyway.

"I still dream about it sometimes," he says grimly. "About building that whole damned factory from scratch myself in a single night. I could have done it too, at the time. You did everything, even the unthinkable. You were a tool, a thing, *Reichseigentum,* a chattel of the German Reich. And as soon as you grew too weak to work at the regulation rate, as soon as you threatened not to be worth that miserable bread ration any longer, they pensioned you off—that's to say forever and six feet under. I kept my mind concentrated on that all the time, never let my attention wander for a single second.

"The *Arbeitskommando,* the work detail I belonged to, was made up mostly of doctors and lawyers and other people who'd never done any manual labor before. Not a day went by without an accident, especially when we were working on the roof. We had to lug heavy concrete beams up a narrow plank propped up steeply against the wall. We'd go up in groups of six, one after the other, like hens. If one of us fell, all the others would lose their balance and everything came crashing down. And anyone not breaking every bone in his body when he hit the ground was given expert assistance in finishing the job by the SS.

"One day I discovered an old friend in the *Kommando,* a man I'd known way back in my student days. His parents had been filthy rich, and he used to pass his old suits on to me. Years later I still looked good in them. I was really pleased to see a familiar face. We had been taught by the same professors, we had danced with the same girls, and now the same SS-men turned out to be after our blood. How about that for destiny?

"I went up to him to shake his hand.

" 'Jacques!' I said. But he ducked away behind a mountain of rubble.

" 'Who are you?' he said. 'You scare me.'

"A Czech from his block told me that he'd cracked up soon after he arrived in the camp."

"What about later on?" Simon asks hopefully. "Did he remember you then?"

"No, he never recognized me. And I didn't want to press the point. Whenever anyone spoke to him, he'd start quaking with fear. I tried to stay as close to him as I could under the circumstances.

"Not that it did any good. One day, when nobody was watching, he managed to get up on the roof all by himself. Down below, we didn't notice him until it was too late. We just saw him taking a short run and then jumping over the edge."

My father pushes his chair back and sets off on a little trot, stretching his arms out wide. "That's the way he jumped off the roof, like a bird flapping its wings. I'll be damned if he didn't look like Charlie Chaplin. A couple of SS-men shot at him as he was falling, and he dropped out of the sky like a stone." Arms still outstretched, my father stops in the middle of the room. "Oddly enough," he says, looking up at the ceiling, "I keep thinking to this very day that if they hadn't hit him he probably would have flown away. Up, up, and away."

Practice

He made himself a knife in the camp. It lies in the drawer with the rest of the cutlery, but it's never used. It's not an ordinary knife: it doesn't shine, the blade is full of scratches, and the blunt side is bent. But the main difference between this knife and the others is that it has a story to tell.

"I made it out of airplane steel," explains my father. "It took me months to do."

"Were you allowed to have knives?" asks Max.

"Of course we weren't, what do you think? I had to make it on the sly, when the SS weren't looking. I worked on it in the factory because we had tools there. I ground the handle on a lathe, but I filed the blade down by hand. Once it was finished, I always carried it on me. That wasn't easy, because the guards searched us every night."

He jumps to his feet and then stands completely still, arms high in the air, as if an invisible SS-man were frisking him.

"They looked everywhere except in your armpits. So I would slip the knife up my sleeve and make sure it stayed caught in my armpit."

"Didn't they ever find it?" Simon asks.

"I wouldn't be standing here if they had. They weren't stupid. They knew very well a prisoner wasn't going to make himself a knife just to spread butter on his bread. The war was almost over, and the Red Army was getting closer every day. I was convinced that at the last moment, with liberation in sight, they'd murder us, so I prepared myself for the worst."

"Did you kill any SS-men with it?" Max asks eagerly.

"With the knife?" my father says softly. "No, not with the knife."

That sounds mysterious and menacing. We want to hear more, but my mother doesn't give us the chance.

The next afternoon Max takes the knife to the rail-road embankment. He says we've got to practice with it. One after the other we stick our arms up, but when we slide the knife into our sleeves it slips down through our clothes onto the grass. Max is the only one who eventually manages to keep it poised in his armpit for a few moments.

"You have to keep saying to yourself: it must not fall out, it must not fall out!" he explains. "You have to think: if it falls out they're going to shoot me or gas me. Try that, it helps!" We try, but the knife is too quick for us.

"I don't want to be gassed!" Simon shouts indignantly, kicking the knife. Max picks it up.

"You see those scratches?" he says. "A long, long time ago, people used to make weapons out of flint. Those were full of scratches, too." He strokes the blade with his forefinger. "This is a prehistoric knife."

Eichmann

"What a funny father you have," Nellie says, giggling. She looks at me expectantly but I avoid her eyes. What can I say? She knows nothing about hunger or about the SS. Words like *barracks, latrine,* or *crematorium* mean nothing to her. She speaks a different language.

Nellie's father doesn't have camp, he has a bicycle that he rides to the factory, with a lunch box strapped to the carrier.

Her mother wears checked carpet slippers all the time. She skates along, up and down the kitchen, scarcely lifting her feet from the floor. The kitchen is where she lives, between the dirty dishes and her mending. She looks permanently angry, not just at us but at the pans, at the coffee pot, and at the whole world. Her false teeth lie in a little bowl on the draining board. She puts them in only on Sundays, when she goes to church.

"You have a television, don't you?" she says when I come around to the back door after school to ask if Nellie is in. "Then you'll be watching Eichmann, too." The hostility in her voice makes me nervous. I fix my gaze on the doormat. "Don't you know who Eichmann is?"

She skates back and forth angrily. Along the way she noisily pushes a chair under the table and fiddles with the knobs on the stove.

"The man's an animal! They were right to put him in a glass cage. I'd like to kick him to death, that dirty bastard!" She takes a long time wiping her hands on her apron. "We saw it for ourselves on television yesterday. All the Jews were pushed into a truck, and as they were being driven off the gas came on inside. Everybody choked to death. There was a little puppy dog running around making whimpering noises. They flung that poor thing into the truck, too."

She raises her arms to show how it was done, but bumps into a closet.

"Your brain just refuses to take it in!" she says, her toothless mouth wide open. "What harm could a puppy dog do? A little puppy like that isn't Jewish, is he?" Nellie appears, making faces behind her mother's back.

"Hello! Let's go out and play."

"No," I say. "No, I have to get home."

My socks are sliding down, but I don't stop running. When I rush into our living room, the television is on. I can see the glass cage on the screen. There's a bald man with eyeglasses sitting in it. He's talking into a microphone. He doesn't look like an animal, he looks like Mr. Klerk, who sometimes substitutes for our teacher, and who makes us sing *Oh, lovely flowers, sleep ye still?* at the beginning of the lesson.

"Is that Eichmann?" I say, disappointed. "He doesn't look horrible at all, he looks like Mr. Klerk from our school." My father nods.

"He looks like the mailman or the baker. The mailman delivers letters and the baker bakes bread and Eichmann sent masses of people to the gas chamber. He just did his job as others do theirs. It makes you sick."

"Then why are you watching?"

"Because I want to understand. But I understand it less now than I did then."

"Nellie's mother says she'd like to kick him to death." My father laughs.

"With those worn-out slippers of hers?"

He lights a cigarette.

"There are lots of people who'd like to do that," he says. "The papers are full of it: letters sent in by people offering to kill Eichmann. Now that he's defenseless, now that anyone can crush him under the toe of an old slipper. A whole army of volunteers. Where were those heroes when we needed them? I find that harder to understand now than ever."

W o o d s

My father has bought a secondhand car. It's a red
Austin with a black roof and a black hood. It has a friendly
look with its bulbous front, like those cars in cartoons that
can think and speak. "That isn't a car," the children in the
street mock, "it's a coffee grinder!"

"You should have bought an Opel," says our neigh-
bor's son.

"My father doesn't buy anything German," Max
mumbles. I don't know why he's ashamed.

On Sunday morning my father takes Simon and me for a
ride. The sky is blue, and we sit in the back seat. My father

drives us to a duck pond outside town. There's a bridge over the water there. We stand on the bridge and drop stale bread through the railings.

Later on we just drive around, along sandy country roads, past fields full of dusty cows. My father is humming. Suddenly he slows down. He leans his head toward the windshield and brakes. On the right side of the road there's a ditch, and beyond that a narrow, overgrown path leading away.

"Great woods," he says. We nod. He clicks his tongue. "Great woods to escape into. So thick and so deep. They'd never find you there, not the ghost of a chance."

He gets out. We stay where we are and watch him jump across the ditch. Then the woods swallow him up.

"What's he up to?" Simon wonders nervously.

"The usual," I say, "just a little escaping." Simon winds down the window.

"I can't hear a thing. Only birds."

"You can't hear escaping," I whisper. "Escaping has to be done very quietly, otherwise it doesn't work."

"And what about us?" he says.

I start sucking my thumb. What does Simon know about such things? Far away, hidden by all that foliage, my father is running. There are twigs and beetles in his hair. Perhaps he won't come back until after dark, his clothes torn. "Great woods!" he will say, sweaty and out of breath.

But here he is already. He isn't even panting.

"For you," he says. He sticks a handful of blackberries through the window.

"Lucky they didn't find you," I sigh, as he gets ready to start the car. He looks around in surprise.

"Who?"

Pinky

I have never heard Nellie's father sing. He probably doesn't know how.

My father sings every evening. When we leave the table, one by one, after supper, he stays in his chair. He opens his mouth a little and rocks backward and forward, as if pumping his voice up from very deep down. It takes a little while for the sound to come out.

We don't understand his songs. He learned them from fellow-sufferers drawn from every corner of Europe, people who shared barracks or bunks with him, or perhaps a piece of bread. They are dead, they can no longer speak, and they can't hear him. Yet it is for them that he sings. His long, drawn-out Slav vowels float over our heads, but they're not meant for us.

One afternoon Simon and I find a tabby cat in the grass at the bottom of the railroad embankment. He can't walk. When we stroke him we can feel his backbone through his fur. Simon gets a box from the vegetable stand to carry him home in, each of us holding a side.

"What next?" says my mother. "You can't take on the suffering of the entire world."

We don't know what suffering means.

"Can he stay?"

"Until he's better," she says.

We call him Pinky. My father can see there's something special about Pinky.

"He looks the way I did when I came back. I was so scrawny I couldn't lift my feet off the ground. Any pebble on the road, I had to walk around it."

Pinky quickly recovers his strength. At supper, he sits in the corner of the windowsill, diagonally behind my father, and gets fed morsels of meat or fish.

Later, when my father sings his songs, Pinky crawls up his chest and puts both paws around his neck. He stays there, hanging in the same position, purring like an outboard motor.

My father is lucky to have Pinky, who understands more than we ever will.

Little Red Riding Hood

It's a muggy summer evening. We're sitting in the garden making angels-on-horseback in the dark, turning our sticks patiently above the glowing embers of a dying fire. Thin slices of dough are folded around the end of each stick. When they are done, we eat them with butter and sugar. Max makes the most beautiful angels, mine are all crumpled.

"Tell us a story," says Simon.

My father doesn't need time to think.

"Right next to the place where we built that factory," he says, "there were woods. I'd keep sneaking looks there during the day, and at night, on my bunk, I'd plan the most amazing escapes. If I could only reach the woods without being seen, I kept telling myself, I'd get away for sure.

"Not long afterward I found out that the woods that were going to be my salvation were no more than thirty yards deep. And immediately behind them was the *Hundezwinger,* where they trained their dogs. Imagine if I had been able to get away. I would have run straight into the jaws of those bloodthirsty beasts!

"And beasts they were, believe me. I saw them tear prisoners to pieces more than once. Being so weak ourselves, we didn't stand a chance against them. They also got better food than we did, a kind of biscuit made out of crushed bones and blood. It wasn't very solid and tended to crumble when it was being transported. The scraps were emptied from the trucks into a dump at the edge of the woods.

"We went crazy over this stuff. While a few of us would distract the SS guard, by dropping a load of stones, for instance, others would crawl to the dump on their bellies to swipe some of the dog meal. That was dangerous for all concerned. Anyone dropping stones could count on a vicious beating. And stealing meant the gallows. We took turns with the risks.

"We hid the stolen dog food in the empty soup kettles that went back to the camp with us at the end of the day. We would chuck twigs, pine cones, and acorns into them, too, anything that would burn and get the stove in the barracks going.

"When we were marched back at night, the kettles were full to the brim. We made sure that the strongest prisoners, meaning those who had lost the least weight, conserved their energy on the way. Just before entering the camp they would take over the heavy kettles, because only they were able to swing them so nonchalantly, as if they were empty. They swung them to the festive accompaniment of the camp orchestra at the gate that welcomed us home like prodigal sons every night.

"Once in the barracks, we quickly lit the little stove and mixed the dog food with water. It was absolutely foul, covered with thick gobs of mold. When the brew came to the boil, the stink could drive you out of the barracks.

"Everyone was given a portion in his mess tin. I would hold mine at arm's length between mouthfuls to stop myself from throwing up. And I'd wonder then why I had risked my life for such vile slop."

"That isn't a story," Simon grumbles with disappointment. "That really happened."

"Do you want a story then? Okay, have it your way!" says my father. "Little Red Riding Hood is walking with her basket through the woods. Suddenly a vicious dog jumps out of the *Hundezwinger*. 'Hello, Little Red Riding Hood, where are you going?' 'I'm going to see my grandmother,' says Little Red Riding Hood. 'She's in the hospital block with typhus.' "

"No," says Simon, "that's not how it goes."

Homesick

When he sings his songs, it's as if he were missing the camp. What can there be to miss about the camp? He did have friends there, but most of the time he had to lug stones and push heavy wheelbarrows. My father had never built a factory before, and I don't think he'll start a second one in a hurry, he's still worn out from the first.

At night, in the barracks, he would play chess with Alex. "We made the chessmen out of stolen potatoes," he says. "If you chew a potato long enough, you get a soft mass you can more or less mold into shape."

Alex was a dentist from Berlin. Before the war, Storm

Troopers had broken into his office. They'd smashed every-thing to smithereens, then knocked Alex down. "So you're a dentist, are you?" they'd said. "We'll give you some work to do!" And they had stomped on his face with their boots. Ever since, Alex had had a lopsided jaw with just a few teeth in it.

Alex and my father made ambitious plans. The two of them designed a special kind of motorcycle on scraps of paper. They were determined to survive the camp and to emigrate to Brazil, where they would market their motorcy-cle and make their fortunes. Why Brazil? I don't know, per-haps it's a good country for motorcycles. It doesn't really matter because Alex didn't keep his end of the bargain. Long before the liberation he died of typhus in the hospital block.

But friends were rare in the camp. The place was teeming with enemies.

"I got more beatings from Poles than I did from Germans," my father says.

"Weren't the Poles prisoners?" Max asks.

"Yes, they were, but they did everything they could to make themselves popular with the SS. Toadies, that's what they were, just like the Ukrainians. They'd bludgeon their best buddies to death for an extra helping of soup."

My mother gives him a sharp look.

"You shouldn't say things like that."

"Like what?"

"That the Poles and the Ukrainians were bad. What you should say is: the Poles I knew, the Ukrainians I met."

My father makes two fists on the edge of the table.

"Oh yes," he snaps, "stick up for that scum, why don't you!"

When he opens his hands, they start to tremble. A little later, his shoulders and his cheeks are shaking, too. Perhaps he misses his enemies most of all.

Scouts

On Wednesday afternoons Nellie doesn't come to play. That's when she goes to Brownies. Right after lunch, she puts on her uniform. I don't like the skirt or the blouse, but the socks are lovely: they have a tassel on the side.

When Nellie is dressed in her uniform she looks different and behaves differently.

"Look," I point. I've drawn circles with crayon on my spinning top, and when the top is spun hard, the circles merge together.

"I don't have time right now," says Nellie, "I've got to go to Brownies." In passing she kicks my top into the gutter.

"What are you going to do there?" I call, running after her. She turns around and shrugs.

"Sing songs, tracking, all sorts of things. You should ask your mother to let you join too, it costs next to nothing."

"May I join Brownies?" I ask that evening. "Nellie belongs too, it costs next to nothing."

"Out of the question," says my mother. "Even if they paid you."

"But they have songs and tracking," I insist.

"It's not for us. You can always sing songs at home. And tracking is for bloodhounds."

My father looks up.

"What are you talking about?" he asks.

"Girl Scouts," she replies.

He closes his book.

"Long before the war," he says to me, "I went camping in the islands one summer. Every time I picked up my binoculars to look at birds, I would see the boys of the Hitler Youth. They were holding combat exercises on the beach. And who did they exercise with? With Dutch Boy Scouts! All tough guys together, very friendly. 'Unfurl the banners soaked in blood!' they would sing, in German." He pats my cheek. "And that's the kind of club you want to join?"

"It was just because of the tassels," I mumble.

Scouts

"I'm not allowed to join Brownies," I tell Nellie the next day.

"Too bad," she says. "Then you're going to miss a whole lot of things, movies, tracking, things like that. And camp."

"Camp?" I repeat, wide-eyed.

Geese

He can hear them a long way off. I don't know how he does it. The radio is on in the room and trains are going by outside, but he looks up from his book and goes out into the street. We run after him in our stockinged feet.

Honking loudly, a flock of wild geese flies overhead. We watch them until they're invisible. By then we're dizzy and have to lean against the front of the house. But my father is as steady as a rock. Legs wide apart, he continues to stare at the sky long after the geese have gone. Then he goes back inside. He gives my mother a kiss and smiles.

"Why do the geese honk?" Simon asks.

"Because no one can stop them," my father says.

"And what are they saying?"

"They're saying: *We go wherever we like, we go wherever we like!*"

My mother shakes her head.

"Geese honk because otherwise they might lose their way, or bump into each other in the sky," she corrects him.

We prefer my father's answer. We cuddle up to him on the sofa.

"In the camp you could see geese in the fall, too," he says. "They would fly over at dawn, during roll call. We'd be on the assembly ground waiting to be counted by the SS, not just once but ten times, twenty times. Either because the number of prisoners was wrong or just to bully us. You had to stand at attention for hours on end, starved and half-frozen. Whenever a flock of geese like that flew overhead, you would think: perhaps one day I will be as free as they are. You just had to believe in that, against all the odds."

His fingers drum on his knees.

"But sometimes it would drive you mad, the idea that everything was going on as usual. The geese flying overhead, the grass growing, the sun rising, and the Earth turning as if there was nothing wrong." He sighs. "Even a mole in the ground and the lice on my head had more freedom than I did." Simon nods.

"If you'd been a mole, you could have dug a tunnel out of the camp!" he says excitedly.

There's a picture hanging in the classroom, with a label saying *In Field and Meadow*. There are lots of animals in it, including a mole, a black one, with hairs on its nose. It has long pink fingers on its front paws, which look like human hands.

"Don't moles have ears?" I ask.

"They do," says the teacher, "but they're so small you can't see them. Big ears would get in the way of the digging. A mole has to be streamlined."

So there you are. My father is not nearly streamlined enough and would have got stuck underground by his ears. What's more, once he became a mole he would have had to be a mole for the rest of his life. And then how would he ever have come home from the camp? And would my mother have recognized him? "Hello, Ephraim. My, how you've changed."

No, things are never as simple as they seem.

W i l l i

Whenever Nellie goes to the toilet, she looks down between her legs. She's sure there's a crocodile lurking in the water just waiting to bite her. I'm not scared of crocodiles. I'm scared of vermin. What I'm most scared of is Willi Hammer.

"Willi was a *Kapo,* a work boss," says my father. "With a criminal record long enough to paper this room at least twice over. A German criminal who specialized in the raping of minors, but an expert at common assault and murder, too. He must have been about fifty. Bald head, low forehead, and a squint. A squinting caveman. He carried a chain with a lead ball the size of a biggish ping-pong ball at one end. He'd use it suddenly to lay into some prisoner chosen at random, and he wouldn't stop until the man was dead. Everyone shivered in his shoes when he was around.

"Some people—and there will always be this sort of person—sucked up to him. He would make them steal for him and sleep with him. When he got tired of them, their hours were numbered. I remember a Russian boy who worked in the vegetable garden and who stole tomatoes for him. He was in favor for a whole month, and Willi even called him Sweetie. One night we heard the boy screaming, panic-stricken, 'Please don't send me to the gas chamber!'

" 'What do you take me for?' Willi replied. 'The gas chamber is far too impersonal. I think so much of you, Sweetie, I'm going to finish you off with my bare hands!'

"That man was one of the lowest forms of life, on a level with a stinkhorn. Only scum like that could get ahead in the camp. We were completely at the mercy of vermin like him. Willi made us pay for every last thing that had ever been done to him, for all his mistakes, all his humiliations, all his failures. No one had it in for us like Willi Hammer.

"He always picked on me. 'I take a special interest in you,' is how he put it.

"In practice what it amounted to was this. Every night after work he would take me aside and beat me up. He'd leave the lead ball in his pocket and use his bare fists.

Coming from him, that was as good as a compliment, a mark of affection.

"Though he clubbed other prisoners and sent them off to meet their Maker without a second thought, when he laid hands on me he raised beating to a fine art. He'd take careful aim and hit my most vulnerable spots every time. After he'd knocked me to the ground, he'd take a break. Sometimes he'd smoke a cigarette or file his nails, while I picked myself up and stood at attention. I never uttered a sound. I knew instinctively that if I did, he'd lose interest in me and go on beating me until he'd laid me out for good.

"At first I would bite my lips until they bled to keep control of myself. Later on, it was easy. I despised him. True, he could hurt me, but even pain has a limit. I was superior to him. That's why he hated me, that's why he beat me up, and that's why he was attached to me. Where would he have been without me? I gave him a purpose in life, he was as dependent on me as I was on him."

My father looks at his hands and shakes his head slowly.

"He succeeded in the end, too."

"How?" I ask anxiously.

"How?" asks Simon. But we get no reply.

"Vermin," says my father, "lousy vermin."

U g h

Nearly all his books are about Indians. We take a special interest in the names of the chiefs: Black Hawk, Crazy Horse, Ten Bears, Red Cloud.

We watch Westerns on television, in which Indians on horseback chase trains or long lines of covered wagons. They make war whoops and wave their tomahawks. Sometimes they attack a fort, to scalp the palefaces. The wives of the palefaces try to get away but keep tripping over their long skirts. They get carried off to the Indian village and tied to a pole. We feel sorry for them, but my father says it's their own fault.

"Once upon a time," he says, "all America belonged

to the Indians. One tribe lived on fish, another on buffalo, and there was enough room and enough food for everybody. Until the settlers came and chased the Indians out.

" 'Why do we have to go?' the Indians asked. 'We've lived here for centuries, our ancestors are buried here.'

" 'We're not exactly enjoying this either,' said the settlers, 'but it can't be helped. The fact is, we have to have more *Lebensraum,* a whole lot more *Lebensraum.* You'll be resettled on another piece of land. There isn't a lot growing on it, and there are fewer buffalo, but you'll get used to it. Learn to grin and bear it.'

"So the Indians grinned and bore it, and they made a long journey on foot to their new dwelling place. They had hardly pitched their tents and lit a fire when the settlers were back.

" 'Out of the way!' they shouted. 'We're building a railroad through your hunting grounds. Pack up your tents, because this is where we're going to put a train station, and perhaps a church and a few houses, too.'

"In the end the Indians were sent off to reservations, to ghettos where they fell sick with grief. Then a white priest showed up, who handed out Bibles.

" 'If you're sick,' said the priest, 'then you must pray to Jesus.'

" 'We already have a god,' the Indians explained. 'His name is The Great Spirit. He makes the sun rise and the grass grow.'

" 'Jesus is mightier,' said the priest, 'Jesus heals.'

" 'Oh really?' said the Indians. 'Then why can't he heal your people? You make false promises, you steal our land, you desecrate our graves, you murder our people. You are much sicker than we are.' "

Max, Simon, and I didn't realize that cowboys are SS-men in disguise. That's probably because they don't speak German and they wear cowboy hats.

That night I dream that my father is an Indian chief. His name is Escaping Wolf. He gallops over the prairie in his underpants, the scars on his chest painted bright red and blue. He is singing Slav songs at the top of his voice. Sitting in front of him on the horse, Pinky meows along, out of tune. The two of them are the terror of the whole Wild West.

Silence

He comes in just after my mother has put bowls of yogurt down in front of us. He stops in the middle of the room and feels around in his coat pockets for a long time, as if he has lost something. Then he looks at her.

"It's acting up again," he says. She nods. "But this time they're not going to operate," he adds quickly. "All I have to do is stay in bed for a while."

She gets up and goes to the kitchen. He follows close behind her and shuts the door. We listen. Even Pinky, who is lying on the windowsill washing himself, pricks up his ears. Pinky's tongue hangs out of his mouth.

Behind the door all is quiet. We wait without knowing what for. What should we do? We can't go on sitting at the table forever, but we can't leave either. Really, we shouldn't be here at all.

After a while, Simon puts his spoon into his yogurt.

"Quiet!" Max hisses. "Didn't you hear it's acting up again?"

"And that means I can't eat my yogurt?" Simon asks.

"No, you can't."

Simon stays where he is, with the spoon in his hand. None of us moves, just like in Sleeping Beauty's castle where everyone has fallen asleep.

When it's dark, my mother comes back into the room. Her bun is askew on the back of her head and her blouse is hanging out of her skirt. She leads us upstairs.

She doesn't even tell us to brush our teeth, she just sits down on Simon's bed and begins to cry. We stand around her in our underwear. Max puts a hand on her shoulder.

"Don't cry," he says. "You still have me, don't you?"

She wipes her tears away. Hairpins fall to the floor.

"Does Papa have to go back to the camp?" I ask, as she tucks me in.

"No, he's sick and he's not going to get better staying here with us. He's going somewhere else to get well again. As soon as he's better, he'll come home."

Silence

"I miss him already," I say.

She gives me a kiss. "Always remember: tomorrow is another day."

I shut my eyes tight. Tomorrow is another day, but I want to sleep for a hundred years. Then, when I wake up, my father will be back. There'll be paper chains in the room and we'll be eating cake. "In the camp," he'll say, "I had bread made out of sawdust." He'll smile. He will never leave us again.

Horror Stories

"What's tuberculosis?" I ask Simon. We are looking for Pinky, who hasn't been seen since the day my father left for the sanatorium.

"A disease in your lungs," Simon says. "You get it from germs, little bugs that Papa swallowed in the camp. He ate grass, too. When you're hungry you'll eat anything."

I look at the coarse grass on the railroad embankment with revulsion.

"I wouldn't."

Simon laughs.

"Just you wait, when there's a war you'll be glad to have a plate of grass!"

"There won't be any war!"

"Oh, yes, there will," says Simon. "You can feel it in your bones."

I feel nothing at all.

"When will it start?" I ask, to be on the safe side.

My brother shrugs.

"Tomorrow afternoon? Next week? It may have started already, you can never tell with wars."

"And what do we do when it starts?"

"I told you: we hide in the cellar and eat grass." The cellar is pitch dark and smells of dampness.

"How long do we have to stay there?"

"Maybe a year," says Simon. "But it could easily be longer, just think of the Eighty Years' War. Before we go into hiding, we have to pick a sackful of grass."

"Just one? Is that enough?"

"Two, then, or three. When the grass is gone, we'll slaughter Pinky."

In my mind's eye I can see Pinky sunning himself on the windowsill. I get a lump in my throat.

"Are you sure?"

Simon nods.

"With a knife," he says. "I'm quite sure."

"Mama will never allow it!"

"She'll have to, it's a case of survival. In war, people are more important than animals. We're lucky to have a cat.

The neighbors have a canary, there's a lot less meat on that."

I don't feel sorry for the neighbors, I feel sorry for Pinky. My eyes fill with tears. Simon puts an arm around me.

"I don't like it any better than you do," he says, "but it can't be helped. You'll see, it won't be that bad. Cat tastes just like chicken, you can't tell the difference."

Sobbing, I push him away.

I walk home with heavy steps. When I enter the room, my mother is sitting at the table with Pinky on her lap.

"Hush now," she says soothingly to me, as she strokes the cat's dappled head, "he's back."

I follow the movements of her hand through my tears. I hate my mother. She looks like the witch from the gingerbread house, feeling Hansel to see if he's fat enough yet to be baked in her oven. I stand by helplessly. "Gretel wept bitter tears," it says in Grimm's *Fairy Tales,* "but all in vain."

Request

It's cold in his room. Although it's been snowing, the window is wide open.

"Hello, Ephraim," says my mother, taking books and clean clothes from her bag.

My father is wearing a thick cardigan sweater over his pajamas. I'm not allowed to give him a kiss, but I may sit on his high bed, which is next to the window. He points.

"I put out nuts every day for the titmice. They fly into the room, too, and sometimes I feed them on the bed."

"Here?" I ask incredulously.

"Yes, just look, they've picked little bits of thread from the bedspread. They're so tame they practically eat out of your hand."

I look at the nuts on the windowsill and at the snow-covered pine trees in the distance. I'm proud of my father. The titmice don't visit other people with bugs in their lungs, they make sure not to. But they flock onto his bed, crowding each other away to take food from his hand.

When visiting time is over, a nun comes up to us in the corridor. She strokes my head and takes my mother aside.

"Your husband suffers from insomnia," she says. "He spends all night long wandering. We can't get him back into bed. Then when he finally does fall asleep, he has nightmares and shouts so loudly you can hear him all over the building. When we come in to see what's going on, we find him fighting with his sheets." She makes gestures in the air. "He wrings his pillow between his hands and won't let go, as if he's trying to choke somebody," she says reprovingly. "The lack of sleep and the excitement are bad for him. Besides, he sweats, so he gets chilled." My mother nods.

"He does that at home, too."

"In that case," the nun says, "you might have warned us. To avoid misunderstandings."

My mother looks at the floor. Then she pulls at the nun's sleeve.

"My husband has camp."

"Camp?" the nun repeats, eyebrows raised. In the long corridor, the word has a hollow echo.

"Concentration camp. That's why he has those

Request

nightmares. At home he doesn't have them every night. But here, in strange surroundings. . . . And he misses us so much. Couldn't you make an exception for him?"

"Concentration camp," says the nun. "We can give him a sleeping pill, of course. We'll do our best."

"I wish I had titmice on my bed, too," I say, when we are sitting in the train.

My mother does not respond. Her gaze passes over my head, out of the window.

"They'll do their best," she says, "they'll do their best."

Thimble

"You went into hiding during the war, too, didn't you?" Max asks my father. He is leaning forward in bed while my mother plumps up his pillows. He nods.

"First in the countryside," he says, "and later in town, in a house in Adelbert Kennis Square."

"Adelbert Kennis, who was he?"

"I have no idea, I only know his statue. It was made of bronze. The local housewives regularly scrubbed the pigeon droppings off his head and shoulders. Adelbert came through the war spotless, not a hair on his head was hurt."

"Where did you hide?"

"Behind a trapdoor in the attic. You could hardly turn around in there. I'd slip out sometimes at night, and only very rarely during the day. But mostly I sat in my hiding place, like a giant in a thimble."

"Was it really that small?"

"About the size of our kitchen sink unit, but taller. There was a child's mattress, it only just fit in."

"And what did you do there?"

"I looked at the roof tiles and thought of Mama's legs."

"The whole time?"

"When I wasn't thinking of her legs, I would read. The people I was hiding with went to the library for me every week. They brought me books on the craziest subjects, but I was happy with anything."

"Did they give you food, too?"

"They didn't have much, but what they had, they shared with me. The man worked in the docks. He had a moustache and enormous hands. I remember the Christmas dinner best. Weeks beforehand he announced that he'd got hold of a rabbit on the black market for Christmas. He was so excited that he mentioned it to everyone and anyone. Christmas came. The rabbit was roasting. I could smell it in the attic, my mouth began to water. At lunchtime, the door-bell rang. I crept back into my hiding place and waited for the visitors to leave. I'd just come out when the bell rang again. That went on till evening. The man had advertised his rabbit so well that the whole neighborhood came by for a taste. In the end, all that was left for me was a paw with a miserable little bit of meat on it. For days I sucked on it."

When we get home from our visits to the sanatorium we have to go straight to bed. But this time I run into the kitchen and open the cupboard under the sink. The smell of damp cloths comes up to meet me. I bend down. There sits my father, cross-legged in the dish rack with the dishcloth around his neck. He's thinking of my mother's legs. Cheerfully he waves a rabbit's knucklebone. I wave back. "Good night, Papa."

Barracks

"What happened to your nativity scene?" my mother asks. My father makes a sad face.

"I hid some nuts under the straw, for the titmice," he tells us. "When they flew into the room they turned the whole thing upside-down, manger and all, just as Sister Benedicta came in. She gave a shriek and demanded to know what was going on. I said, 'Well, it looks as if the little creatures aren't believers.' So she took the nativity scene away in a huff. Luckily I still have my angel."

He points to a pine branch, from which the plaster figure of an angel hangs by a ribbon. The mouth is painted wrong. The red isn't on the lips, but above them. It's an angel with a bloody nose, and he's carrying a dusty pennant with *Gloria* written on it.

Simon doesn't say a word. He won't sit on the bed but stands next to it and doesn't take his eyes off my father. Max walks up and down the room looking bored. He drags his feet one after the other across the gray linoleum.

"Why don't you all go outside for a while?" suggests my mother. "You, too, Simon. But make sure you do what Max tells you."

We trudge down a wide flagstone path toward the woods behind the sanatorium. On the way we pass a snow-covered lawn where little wooden sheds with sloping roofs are arranged in a semicircle. They look deserted. That doesn't surprise me, because they have only three walls and are open on one side, like the doll house at school. Who would want to live in a house where it snows indoors? Max heads straight for them, but Simon holds me back.

"Don't do it!" he shouts to Max. "They're barracks!"

Hand in hand we wait at the edge of the lawn, while Max goes into the nearest little house. He taps the wood like an expert. Then he bounces up and down to test the floor. Tears are running down Simon's cheeks. I hold my breath. "Crybaby," says Max when he rejoins us, quite unharmed. He gives Simon's back a shove that sends him sprawling in the snow.

Barracks

"In the afternoon," my father explains to Max later, "patients rest in there and fill their lungs with fresh air. Those little houses are cleverly designed. They're on a plinth and can be swiveled out of the wind. They take four beds each."

Max gives Simon and me a scornful look.

"Barracks!" he whispers. "Barracks!"

Tarpaulin

"The time I spent at Jeff's was the best," he says. "There were five of us in hiding on his farm, way out in the middle of nowhere. I was called Bart there."

A breeze blows through the open window. My father, wearing a scarf, is sitting up in bed. Wisps of black hair dance in front of his eyes.

"Jeff was a man of few words. Slight but wiry, a little stooped, cap on one side of his head. One afternoon when we were out in the fields we heard a plane far away in the distance.

" 'Bart,' Jeff said to me, 'you've got to explain to me exactly how that thing manages to stay up in the air.'

"He turned his hoe upside down and rested his chin on the blade. He could listen for hours. Whenever he wanted to know something, he had all the time in the world. And he wanted to know everything, just everything. While Europe was being reduced to ashes, Jeff leaned on his hoe and asked about the law of gravity or about Louis Pasteur.

"For safety's sake we slept in a pit in the woods. That was no problem in the spring and the summer, but in the autumn it began to pour. Our pit started filling up with rainwater, and we needed a tarpaulin to cover it.

" 'I don't have one,' said Jeff, 'try asking Verdonck.'

"Verdonck was a farmer up the road who had gone to school with Jeff. He knew us. Every Sunday he would come visiting in his Sunday best. Then he and Jeff would reminiscence and even Jeff would laugh.

"It so happened that Verdonck did have a piece of tarpaulin. It was lying on the floor of his cowshed and had seen better days, but it would do for us.

" 'How much do you want for it?' I asked.

" 'Four hundred guilders,' he said. That was a ridiculous sum for an old tarpaulin. We didn't have that sort of money.

" 'Well?' Jeff asked that evening. I shook my head.

" 'Too steep.'

" 'How much did he want for it?'

" 'Four hundred guilders.'

"So that's how things were left until the next Sunday, when Verdonck came to pay his weekly visit. Jeff was waiting for him at the door.

" 'Verdonck,' he said calmly, 'if I ever see you here again, I'll sic the dog on you.'

"One night soon afterward we heard Germans in the woods. Three of us were caught. I managed to get away to the fields in the dark, dived into the first haystack I came across, and landed on a plow stored under the hay."

"Is that how you got those scars on your legs?" Max asks. My father nods.

"I jumped straight into the blades." He falls back onto his pillows.

"No need for them to beat their swords into plowshares for my sake," he says, "God forbid!"

Homecoming

My mother is wearing a new skirt. There are poppies on it. They dance when she moves, like the poppies in the tall grass at the bottom of the railroad embankment.

We've tied a red ribbon in a bow around Pinky's neck. Confused, he chews at the long loops.

"Leave him be," says my mother, "Pinky's handsome enough as he is."

From school, we race straight back home. My mother is standing in the street with one hand over her eyes.

"I can't imagine where he is," she says. We take up positions next to her and peer at the same point in the distance, as if our combined stares could make him appear by magic. When that doesn't work, we grow bored. We run around, push each other, go and sit on the curb, and get up again listlessly.

"Can't we have some cake while we're waiting?" Max nags. My mother shakes her head.

"Pinky licked all the whipped cream off the cake. He's stuffed himself and right now he's sleeping it off on the windowsill. If you squeezed him, the cream would come out of his nose. We could try that, to resurrect the cake, but I don't think it would taste very good."

"Damn," says Max.

"I used to have a cake cover," my mother says, "before you went and caught tadpoles with it."

We go on waiting until the sun rolls off the railroad embankment like a big orange sour ball. Then, halfway down the deserted street, my father appears. Where did he spring from so suddenly? With his flaming red face and his flaming shoulders he looks like the prophet Elijah come down from heaven in a fiery chariot. We stand there blinded and don't even raise our limp arms in greeting.

"Are you smoking again?" my mother asks reproachfully. We're sitting in the garden, under the poplars where the chirping birds have fallen silent.

"I bought a whole carton," he says, indicating his

suitcase in the grass. "When my train came in this morning, I broke into a cold sweat. I don't know what got into me. I walked up and down the platform all day smoking cigarettes. I let train after train go by. I was afraid to get in. Crazy, eh?"

My mother, who is about to pour us coffee, clasps the pot to her chest. The poppies on her skirt hold their breath.

"Look," Max exclaims. Pinky has raised himself up to his full height inside the window and is scratching at the glass as if trying to dig his way through.

"Go quickly and open the door for him," says my mother.

Max and Simon run inside. A moment later, Pinky leaps into my father's arms.

"Hello, my friend," says my father, "I'm a little late."

Heaven

"Why don't you people ever go to church?" Nellie asks. "Don't you have one?"

"I don't think so."

"Don't you believe in the Trinity?" I look down at my shoes in embarrassment. There's a fish dealer at the market. Near closing time he always calls out, "Two for the price of one, two for the price of one!" The Trinity is probably three for the price of one, but three of what? "Or in Our Dear Lord?" Nellie insists.

"My father's fallen out with him."

"What about?"

"About the war."

Heaven

This time it's Nellie who's at a loss for words. Falling out with Our Dear Lord, she's never heard of such a thing.

"If you don't go to church, you won't go to heaven either," she says. That seems a pity to me.

"There's a christening in the church this afternoon. I have to sing there. I'll ask if you can join us," she says magnanimously.

"Will I go to heaven then?"

"Maybe."

We stroll to the church together. It's much bigger inside than it looks from the street. A sweet smell hangs in the air. Two boys laugh as they chase each other through the vestibule and splash water from a font on the wall with their hands. Nellie sniffs disapprovingly.

"That's a sin," she whispers. "Holy water is sacred."

I follow her down an aisle through the nave. There are paintings of Jesus carrying an enormous cross on his bare back.

"Look at that," I point, "he's all orange!"

"Of course, he is," says Nellie. "That's because he suffered."

"My father isn't orange."

"Your father wasn't crucified, was he?"

"No, but he did suffer."

"Then he obviously didn't suffer enough," she says with conviction.

We come upon the priest in a side room, standing beside a group of children. He gives us a friendly nod, then hands out sheets of paper with the words of a song written on them. We practice it twice. *"The Lord is my shepherd,"* we sing, *"I shall not want."* It makes no sense.

"What?" I whisper, nudging Nellie. "What shall I not want?"

"It means you're not going to need anything," she snaps.

When the christening ceremony is over, the priest reaches into a deep tin box and gives each of us a stick of licorice and a piece of chewing gum wrapped in striped paper.

"I was christened Petronella Johanna Maria," says Nellie, when we skip home. "What about you?"

"I wasn't christened," I say. She freezes.

"You weren't christened? Oh, but then you can't go to heaven at all. They'll never let you in!"

I give her a scornful look. Then, clutching my candy, I turn and run off. I shall not want.

Dance Class

Max has been getting himself ready for his first dance lesson. His black hair, which usually has a big lock hanging halfway down to his cheek, is combed slickly back. He's wearing a shirt and a tie.

"Remember," my mother says, as she straightens his jacket, "to do up your button when you ask a girl to dance."

My father puts down his book.

"In the camp," he says, "the summers claimed more victims than the winters. There was dust swirling around everywhere, we were thirsty the whole time, and everyone got sick. There was one mysterious epidemic. From one moment to the next, people who appeared to be in good health lost consciousness. Hundreds of them were dragged away and covered by a big tarpaulin, where they died a few days later.

"My friend Anton had the dubious honor of being one of the first, so at least he was given a place in the hospital block. One Sunday afternoon I found out that he was near the end. I badly wanted to see him one last time, but prisoners couldn't just go and visit the sick if they wanted to. You needed a special permit, a so-called *Schein*, which was very hard to get. My chances were especially slim because our block leader at the time was Sigismund the Flogger. Sigi was not the sort of man you would think of approaching at all, let alone with a request, but I decided to take the risk.

" 'What do you want a *Schein* for?' he asked suspiciously.

" 'To visit a sick friend in the hospital block,' I said. He grabbed the gigantic steel soup ladle that was hanging from his belt as usual, then used the handle to scratch the back of his head.

" 'If I were to give you a going over with my ladle,' he grinned, 'you wouldn't need a *Schein*. You'd be in the hospital block yourself!'

" 'I'm aware of that,' I said, 'but I'd rather go there under my own power.'

Dance Class

"Promptly he ordered the whole block to fall in. He did so quite often when he was about to crush someone's skull because he liked having an audience for his little excesses. So I braced myself for the worst, but to my surprise he hooked the ladle back onto his belt.

" 'You damned rabble!' he yelled at the others standing in line. 'All you ever think of is yourselves! Let this boy be an example. He comes to me, to Sigi the Flogger no less, to ask permission to visit a sick pal. That's what I call a *real* comrade!'

"He put his arm around me protectively.

" 'But I can't possibly send him through the camp looking the way he does. That would really go against my principles. Here he is, just back from doing outside fatigue duty, and he hasn't got a decent stitch to his name. You over there!' he shouted, pointing to a prisoner. 'Those pants of yours will do. And you there, you won't miss your jacket for a few hours. Hand them over!'

"When he had decked me out from head to toe in new things, he said, 'Come on, then.' In his small room he sat me down in a chair, draped a sheet around me, and lathered my face with real shaving cream. Then he gave me an impeccably smooth shave, and rubbed my face with eau de cologne, just like a first-class barber. Squeaky clean, I finally made my way to the hospital block, while Sigi stood in the barracks doorway following me with his eyes and looking as pleased as a father watching his son going off to his dance class."

He laughs.

"I don't see what's so funny," says Max. "That Sigi was a real bastard, wasn't he?"

"He was a bastard all right, but I hang on to this one good memory of him. I'm entitled to that."

"And what if he had slit your throat with that razor? Or if he'd sent you to the gas chamber in your new clothes?"

"If, if," says my father. "If my grandma had had a beard she would have been my grandpa."

Max leaves the room without saying goodbye. My mother goes to the window to watch him. As he jumps onto his bicycle she makes funny faces and calls out, *"Quick, quick, slow!"* But he doesn't look back.

Stranger

We get to choose between a visit to the circus or going to the movies. I have never been to the circus, but because Simon feels sorry for the elephants and Max doesn't think the clowns are funny, they want to see a film about Odysseus.

"Who's that?" I ask.

"A Greek king," says Max, "who fought against Troy and got lost on his way home."

"And what happened then?"

"Then he met witches and giants. It's very exciting."

If Max says so, it's bound to be true. He's being taught Greek at school by a fat man with a red face.

"We're going to see Odysseus," I tell my mother, who is busy slicing string beans in the kitchen. "It's about a king who got lost."

"That's right," she says. "The gods were angry with him and punished him by making him wander the seas for years. But he couldn't forget his lovely wife, the beautiful Queen Penelope. When he finally returned to Ithaca, no one recognized him." She wipes her hands on her apron. "He had become a stranger," she says slowly, "in the land of his dreams. I had to translate that story at my final exams. I got an *A* for it. The war had only just started."

Since the cinema is being renovated, we get our tickets at half price. Max is beaming all over, because we'll be able to buy ice cream with the extra money.

The auditorium smells of sawdust and paint. Big, wooden scaffolding has been put up in the aisle and on either side of the screen. The seats are hard.

Odysseus doesn't wear a crown, just a short dress with pleats. That wasn't a good idea, because now you can see his hairy knees all the time. He's brave, all right. He sticks a burning tree trunk into the Cyclops's eye. The Cyclops roars with pain and tries to grab Odysseus. Simon and I hold our breath. Luckily Max keeps telling us what comes next. "Soon he's going to hang on to the belly of a ram," he says, "and then he'll escape from the cave." Or, "Any minute now he'll draw his bow and shoot them all dead."

"When I grow up, I want to be a sailor, too," says Simon after the film. Max snorts.

"How're you going to do that when you're scared of water? You're even afraid to take a bath!"

"Only when my hair has to be washed," Simon says indignantly, "because the shampoo gets in my eyes."

The streetlights are already on. We walk quickly home. I push my hand into Max's.

"Papa is just like Odysseus," he says. "Papa was imprisoned by monsters, too."

"That's true," I agree, "but Papa didn't wear a dress."

"True," says Simon. "And Odysseus didn't have lice."

Q u e s t i o n s

"If God exists," says Max, "then why didn't he do anything?"

My father, who has finished eating, lights a cigarette.

"What do you mean?" he asks, blowing smoke out of his nostrils.

"He could have stopped the trains, couldn't he? He could have knocked the camp down with one finger, couldn't he? Why didn't he help you?"

"God isn't some kind of odd-job man," my father smiles. "Imagine if he were there to do our bidding the whole time. What a mess we'd be in then!"

"Aren't you angry with him?"

"Now and then."

"But you still believe in him?"

"You could call it that."

"I think that's stupid!" Max says piercingly. My father sighs.

"You can't blame God. God didn't shout *Sieg Heil!* when Adolf Hitler came to power. God didn't cheer when Europe was trampled underfoot. People like you and me did that. The trains were driven by human beings, the gas chambers were invented by human beings. Of course, those people had been created by God, but they had free will. They could do what they felt like, and it just so happened that they felt like genocide."

"If God created all men, then he created Hitler, too!" says Max triumphantly.

"That's undeniably so," my father replies calmly, "but Hitler was responsible for his own actions."

"And God just let him get away with it?" says Max, aggrieved. "But that's not fair!"

"No one says it's fair. If you want a fair world, you'll have to look for another one."

Max blinks.

"So you believe in some bastard of a God who looks on without raising an eyebrow while everyone's being killed?"

"There's no alternative," says my father. "I'd rather

have a God I can't understand than no God at all. So I'll have to put up with him, for better or worse."

"Suit yourself!" cries Max. "Just don't keep coming to me with stories about that stupid camp of yours. It served you right!"

My father raises his finger, and shakes it threateningly over the dishes.

"I don't like your tone!"

"Oh, no? And what are you going to do about it?"

My mother gets up from the table.

"Be quiet, Max."

"Why don't you hit me then?" Max yells at my father. "Just like the SS!" My mother pulls him off his chair and starts pushing him toward the door. "Kick me to death, why don't you!" Max shouts over her shoulder. "Why don't you gas me!"

Simon is pinching my arm. He's doing his best not to burst into tears. My father gasps for air.

"Come now, Ephraim," says my mother. She lays her hand on his, but he shakes it off and rubs his face.

"What do you all want from me?" he says. "It's hard enough as it is."

Underpants

"You often see pictures of prisoners in striped pajamas," my father says, "but during the last years of the war only the camp hotshots had clothes like that. Some block leaders were the proud owners of a striped jacket. We wore rags considered too shabby even for the Winter Relief.

"We had no shoes. In the beginning we walked around on bits of wood. Later on we went barefoot. They ought to have fitted us with horseshoes, that would have been more practical. For a while I was in the *Kabelkommando*, the outside work party that extracted copper from old electricity cables so it could be used again. The stuff was easy to steal. Back in the barracks you could go on picking at it until you were left with thin strands of wire. If you could lay your hands on a few scraps of cloth somewhere, then you could join them together with the copper wire. It meant you didn't need a needle. It took a lot of patience, but that's how we made ourselves socks, or something that looked like socks from a distance.

"There wasn't any underwear. When I arrived in the camp I still had my own underpants. I wore them backwards and inside out until they were stiff with filth. Now and then I managed to wash them with snow. They fell apart eventually."

"Did you go around with a bare behind then, like a ballet dancer?" Simon asks.

"Ballet dancers don't have bare behinds!" cries Max. "They wear tights!" Simon bursts into tears.

"Once," my father continues, "there was a rumor that we were about to get new underwear. I didn't believe a word of it, but I was evidently mistaken, because after roll call one morning we were marched off to the *Bekleidungskammer,* the clothing stores, where we were issued one pair of underpants each. And what pants! They were brown paper bags with two holes for the legs. At the top they had a piece of string for tying them around your middle. Useless trash, which we had to throw away after a few hours, since all of us had diarrhea and were up to our ears in shit the whole time."

Underpants

Simon wipes his tear-stained cheeks.

"How can you go on living if you don't have underpants?" he says mournfully. My mother strokes his hair. She gives my father a quizzical look. He jumps up and walks around the room.

"Wait a moment," he says, "I've forgotten something! Everyone got those underpants except me. When it was my turn, they were all gone. That's right, I remember now. While the others put on their paper underpants in the snow, I was left empty-handed. Just then the assistant camp commandant, the *Lagerführer* himself, came by. He shook his head and said, 'Impossible! This poor devil's entitled to a pair of underpants, and a pair of underpants he'll have, damn it, even if I have to turn the whole camp upside down to find them!'

" 'But the box is empty!' said the man running the *Bekleidungskammer.*

" 'What!' the *Lagerführer* shouted. 'Are you trying to tell me that the Third Reich is short of a pair of underpants?'

"His hand disappeared into the box, groped about inside, and, as if by magic, came up holding a pair of underpants. These underpants differed in every respect from the paper ones. They were made of blue velvet and came down to your knees. The fly had ivory buttons, each in the shape of a small German eagle."

"Really and truly?" Simon asks. My father nods.

"Those pants were indestructible. Top quality. And that's not all. Within a week they started to talk! I think it was just after I'd been detailed to a forest work party. In any case, it happened in the woods. We had to dig pits, the ground was frozen solid, and the handle of my shovel snapped in half. When the guards saw that, they nearly kicked me to death. As if that was any help! I went on working with a broken shovel, and then those underpants suddenly addressed me."

"What did they say?" I ask.

"They spoke in German," says my father. "I don't feel like translating all of it right now, but one of the things they told me was that they answered to the name of Heinrich and that they had once belonged to Adolf Hitler. They'd been looking up Adolf's asshole for years and had learned the most confidential state secrets that way. Then, one day, they were arrested and sent to the camp because they knew too much."

"Talking underpants? But that can't be true!" says Simon. My father raises his hands helplessly.

"Heinrich couldn't believe it himself! He had never tried to speak before, the thought had never even occurred to him. But once he found he could talk, there was no stopping him. And what a lot of talking we did, Heinrich and I! The Nazis were bastards. But their underpants? I won't hear a word said against them!"

"What happened to Heinrich?" we ask.

"By the end of the war I had grown so skinny the underpants didn't fit any more. They kept falling down around my ankles. One day they were picked up by the wind and carried away high, high up into the air.

" 'Heinrich!' I shouted. 'Come back!'

" 'No,' Heinrich called down, 'the view from up here is much too beautiful!'

" 'What can you see?' I asked.

" 'Everything, everything,' Heinrich replied. 'All of Europe. I can even see the future. I can see bread on the table and I can see that girl with the black braids you've been telling me about. And children, I can see children, too.'

" 'How many?' I yelled up, but I couldn't hear Heinrich anymore, he had grown as small as a kite that's broken its string."

Simon still finds it hard to believe.

"Clothes can't talk," he says while we're getting undressed. Max, who doesn't have to go to bed for a long time, leans against the closet.

"Why not?" he says. "Crazier things happened in the camp, people were gassed there." Simon shrugs his shoulders.

"Of course people were gassed there," he says. "That's what a camp is for, isn't it?"

Coincidence

"You were never given a bunk to yourself, that was considered a waste of *Lebensraum*," says my father. "You slept in twos at the very least. After a while the fellow who shared your bunk would disappear to another barracks, or to the hospital block, or to a mass grave. His place would be taken by someone new.

"One morning the old Romanian fellow who had shared my bed for a month was lying against me as cold as a block of ice. His clothes, including a superb pair of socks that by rights I should have inherited, had already, to my regret, been pulled off his body. That night his place was taken by a Dutchman. That was an improvement, because the Romanian had been able to communicate only in sign language and the few scraps of German he had picked up in the camp. But the Dutchman and I struck up a conversation right away. We discovered that we had lived in the same street in The Hague, and, what's more, at the same time. When I mentioned my house number, he said, 'Impossible! That's where I lived!'

" 'Well, it's true,' I said. 'I rented a room from the widow Bosch, first floor front.'

"He slapped his knees in surprise.

" 'I was on the second!'

" 'Then you must have been that waiter from The Golden Swan the widow mentioned. You always got home long after midnight. I often heard you on the stairs.'

" 'That's right,' he said, 'I worked long hours.'

" 'So if you'd fallen through the floor, you'd have landed right in my bed,' I exclaimed, 'and now, damn it, we're sharing a bunk!' "

My father shakes his head. We laugh.

"But a much stranger coincidence happened soon after the liberation. The Red Army put us in a school that was being used as an emergency hospital. There was more emergency in that hospital than anything else, because the Russians had no medicines. We did get three meals a day, though, and a bed to ourselves. We couldn't get over our good fortune.

"There was a locker beside each bed. All the lockers were empty except mine. When I opened the little door I found a book inside that someone must have left behind. I was astounded to find it was *Job*, by Joseph Roth. I'd been carrying a copy of it in my pocket the day I was arrested. It was the last book I laid eyes on before leaving for the camp, and the first I got hold of after the liberation. All I had to do was to look up the page I'd stopped at and I could go on reading, after all those abysmal years, as if nothing had happened."

He takes a book from the bookcase and waves it.

"Look. I brought it home as a memento!" When he puts it down, Simon starts eagerly to leaf through it, but his face clouds.

"It's all dirty!"

My father nods.

"Its last owner must have had blood on his fingers when he read it."

We are shocked. In the margin we can see a dark thumb print that looks like the scab on a wound. "Ugh," says Simon, pushing the book away to the furthest edge of the table. "All I wanted was to see if it had any pictures."

"Pictures of what?"

"I don't know. Of people being liberated by Russian tanks, of everybody cheering."

Coincidence

My father picks up the book and opens it up like an accordion.

"These are the only pictures in it," he says.

Bloodstains swirl over us. The air is leprous with them.

Retarded

"What do you want to be when you grow up?" our teacher asks.

"Invisible," I say. "So the SS won't catch me."

It's the wrong answer. Other hands go up. The teacher points, but everyone shouts at once.

"A captain!"

"A nurse!"

"A fireman!"

When I talk about the war, the teacher acts as if I'm retarded. Hans, who lives in our street, is retarded. He has a big head and a look of surprise, and he drools a little all the time. One day Hans disappeared. Some young bullies had tied him to a tree. He wasn't found until it was dark. There are lots of trees at the bottom of the railroad embankment. Each tree I look at makes me wonder if it's the one they tied Hans to.

One Sunday I went to High Mass with Nellie and her parents. The church was crammed with people. Suddenly Hans turned up in the center aisle. He lay down on the black marble floor and disappeared from view under the front pew. Soon after, he popped up at the other end of the pew, but immediately dropped down again. Weaving from side to side, he crawled under every pew. It was deathly quiet, the acolytes tinkled their little bells, and the priest held up a golden chalice. And Hans burst out singing "Pussycat, pussycat, where have you been?" so loudly that everyone could hear. I nearly wet my pants laughing, but Nellie gave my thigh a vicious pinch.

When we were walking home after Mass, her father said, shaking his head, "Do you know that he grabbed onto my feet? What's that boy doing in church? Children like that ought to be in an institution!"

Hans doesn't belong in church and I don't belong in school. I make our teacher nervous. One day she stopped me by the coat racks and said, "We simply have to get over this war business once and for all." What does she mean by that? She herself goes on and on about war. "Louis of Nassau cut the Spaniards to ribbons at the battle of Heiligerlee," she tells us proudly, as if she had been there to help him. Or, "In 1628, our hero Piet Heyn captured the Spanish Silver Fleet." Or, "The Duke of Alva spread death and destruction through the Low Countries."

There weren't any camps in the seventeenth century, but there was plenty of shooting. One of the pictures in our history book shows Balthasar Gerards shooting Prince William of Orange from such close range that the barrel of his pistol can be seen disappearing into William's belly. A big cloud of smoke is rising out of the hole in the prince. You can't tell if it's from the gunpowder or because William has just eaten a roast turkey. He doesn't look starved, though, and there is no sign of barbed wire. Yet the teacher has tears in her eyes.

Later on we have to draw a portrait of the Duke of Alva in our exercise book. To please the teacher, I give him cruel lips and a bloodthirsty look. When I've finished, she points to the little black square under his nose and exclaims, "What a wonderful moustache he has!" I don't dare tell her that it's Adolf Hitler's.

Soccer

"What was the worst thing about the camp?" Max asks. My father sighs.

"Are you giving me a quiz?"

"No, I just want to know."

"Questions like that are silly," says my father. "Which was worse, the hunger or the bullying, the cold in the winter or the heat in the summer? Was being gassed worse than being hanged? Who can say? Not me, anyway."

"Why not?"

"Because it serves no purpose. Everything was dreadful and appalling. I don't even want to think about it, it's almost indecent to do so."

"Indecent?" says Max with a catch in his voice.

"An insult," says my father, "to everyone who died there."

"I see, so you think I'm insulting?"

My father grips him by the arm.

"Now, you just listen carefully to what I have to say. I don't know exactly what ideas you're getting into your head, but there's one thing you've got all wrong. I love you all, each and every one of you, and you perhaps most of all."

"It's not true!" shouts Max. "All you love is your SS! When we're at the dinner table, you go on about starvation. When we have a cold, you go on about typhus. Other fathers play soccer in the street with their kids, but when I bring a friend home just once, all you can do is talk about the camp. The camp this, the camp that, always the camp. Why didn't you damn well stay there!"

My father lets go of him. At the same moment my mother strides into the room.

"What was that you were saying?" she demands.

"You heard me," mumbles Max.

"Yes, I did, but I couldn't believe my ears. Maybe," she says, lips quivering, "that's because I chose your father from a good thousand fathers. Maybe that's because I thought he was dead, and because after the liberation I spent weeks standing in line at the Red Cross to make inquiries." She is laughing and crying at the same time.

"Luckily I have you to tell me how stupid that was. The man can't even play soccer! If only I'd known that at the time!"

"All I did was ask what was the worst thing about the camp," Max says defensively. "Nothing I do is ever right."

"So if I answer your question," says my father, "can we forget the rest and go back to being normal with each other again?" He is standing by the window, with his back toward us. His fingers drum on the windowsill.

"The worst thing for me," he says, "was when the wind blew across the assembly ground from the crematorium. Because as you stood there, stiffly at attention, the grease carried along on the wind stuck like Vaseline to your cheeks. Do you understand what I'm saying?"

"Yes," says Max, "I understand."

He stands there a little longer, looking down at the mat, then shambles off toward the door.

"And we did play soccer, too, Max. Now and then, on festive occasions, the Poles would play the Greeks, for instance. Or the Czechs would play the Hungarians. The teams were made up of prisoners specially selected beforehand. The weakest would be kicked like straw dolls all over the field by the stronger ones, and we would sometimes have to bury them at halftime. They never asked me to play, they must have realized I was no good at soccer."

"Just leave those building blocks," my mother says to us, "we're going for a short walk."

As we walk down the hallway, we can hear Max howling in his bedroom. We can still hear him down in the street. Only when we have turned the corner does an icy silence descend.

No End

"Istvan was a Hungarian gypsy, nicknamed Rudolph Valentino. He had jet-black eyebrows, more sharply defined than if they'd been painted on. We shared a bunk in a fraternal way, as well as a lot of fat lice that commuted between his rags and mine in a continuous stream of rush-hour traffic. He spoke in a lilting dialect, most of which I couldn't understand. Even the few words of German he had picked up from the SS sounded melodious in his mouth.

"Although he wasn't a member of the camp orchestra, he owned a fiddle, and would play many a czardas for us in the evenings. The block leader loved to listen and would reward him with a piece of bread or some leftover soup, half of which Istvan always passed on to me. If a violin string broke during one of his performances, he'd pull a handful of brand new ones out of his pocket, cool as a cucumber. He was amazing, he could steal an egg out of a hen's backside before she even knew she was going to lay.

"He could swipe the most outlandish things, from blue suede shoes to real caraway cheese. Once he even pinched a compass for us to use during our escape. Because escape we surely would, in a week or a month, no doubt, according to Istvan. I would nod in agreement, but only halfheartedly. Escape was as good as impossible. Whoever tried it usually didn't get very far. The dogs would pick up his scent and when he was returned to the camp he'd be strung up. Sometimes, as a little joke, the SS would dump the fugitive's corpse onto a chair and hang a notice around his neck reading 'Back Again!' I'd been a prisoner long enough to understand that the chances of survival on the other side of the barbed wire were not much greater than they were inside. Istvan didn't know that, or didn't want to know. Every night he sat bent over the compass like a child, seeing in it not just the cardinal points but the whole wide world: forests, mountains, rivers. Even the stars and the planets were mirrored in his dark eyes.

"At the time, my *Arbeitskommando* had the job of unloading stones. It worked like this. One of the prisoners would stand on a truck and throw the stones at top speed to another prisoner standing below, who would catch them and pass them on to the next in line. The catcher at the bottom of the truck had the worst of it, and at night his hands were as raw as fresh steak. Willi Hammer, with his peculiar sense of humor, made me the catcher time after time, until every nerve in my fingers was exposed and small cauliflower-shaped swellings began growing from the bone.

"Other catchers got that too. Skozepa, a Czech, went to the hospital block with it. When he came back, he had no more swellings but no more fingers, either: they'd been cut off with a pair of rubber-cutters. Before he was gassed, we fed him bread with a finger-thick layer of beet-root jam on it, something nobody begrudged him.

"A few days later, a beaming Istvan pushed a small bundle toward me that turned out to contain a tube of sulfur ointment, some clean rags, and a large safety pin. The safety pin was my salvation: I held it in the fire, tore my festering fingers open from top to bottom and dislodged the cauli-flowers one by one."

My father places his hands palms up on the table. We know those thin scars pointing like arrows to the scar tissue on his fingertips, but we look all the same.

"Istvan," he says, "Istvan." He shakes his head slowly. "I don't know what got into him all of a sudden. He abandoned all hope of escaping. He stopped making music. Night after night he sat in a corner of the barracks staring in front of him. 'I can see no end to it,' he would say dejectedly, 'no end, no end.'

"He became reckless, would march out of step, and stole like a magpie. He wouldn't get up on his own in the mornings and had to be clubbed out of his bunk. One morning the inevitable happened.

"I can still remember as if it were yesterday. We were lined up, by blocks, on the snowy assembly ground, standing at attention and ready for inspection by the SS. As soon as the guards showed up, we were supposed to salute them by turning our heads in their direction and removing our caps. The problem was that they always approached from the rear, and we, standing there looking straight ahead, couldn't tell which side they were coming from. To keep mistakes to a minimum, the block leader, who *could* see them coming, had thought up a little ruse. If the SS came from the left he would give the order *'Caps off!'* If they came from the right, he would just shout *'Caps!'* This ploy saved us from a lot of beatings and punishment drill.

"On this particular morning, Istvan was about six rows in front of me, standing rigidly in line like everybody else. We could hear the SS boots. *'Caps off!'* came the command. In unison we looked over our left shoulders and bared our heads. Then there was an ominous silence. Thinking that some idiot had turned the wrong way, I glanced at the other rows out of the corner of my eye."

No End

In the course of telling this story, my father has risen to his feet. He is standing stiffly at attention beside his chair, an invisible cap in his right hand. Slowly he raises this hand and points a finger at a spot in the room where we can see absolutely nothing. His face begins to glow.

"Just imagine," he says, "those rows of prisoners, shaven heads as far as the eye could see. And right in the middle there stood Istvan with, and God alone knows where it had come from, a red tin toy car on the top of his bald head. The thing was held on with bits of string, violin strings probably, which ran from the little wheels down to Istvan's chin, under which he had knotted the ends.

"It was the only time I was in the camp that I saw the SS speechless. Their surprise didn't last very long, of course, a moment at the most, but a moment during which a single *Untermensch*, just one 'subhuman,' made a laughingstock of the whole Third Reich while standing stiff as a ramrod, not moving a muscle, until they dragged him out of the lines.

"Barely half an hour later he was strung up on the gallows before a large audience. We were ordered to march close up to his tortured body and to look at it for two whole minutes. The SS had removed the little red car, as if they were afraid we might go on laughing."

Evacuation

"They're claiming that no one was murdered in the camps," says my father, standing in the kitchen door. He waves the newspaper he has just been reading. "Lies and propaganda, they call it. All those stories about starvation and gas are a pack of lies. We were imprisoned just for the fun of it."

My mother walks back and forth between the sink and the stove.

"They're holding meetings," he says, "and talking big again. They're protected by the same freedom of speech they want to rob us of as soon as they can. Today they grab a finger, *and tomorrow the whole world.*"

Evacuation

My mother is stirring something in a small saucepan.

"Are you listening to what I'm saying?" he asks. She nods.

"Yes, I am, but I don't see them marching yet. And while I wait, I've got a sauce to make for the broad beans." She looks at him. "Why do you keep on reading that sort of thing?" she says fiercely. "You know it upsets you." He sighs.

"So I'm not even allowed to read the papers now! I don't have to shut my eyes to it, do I? I'd like to be told in good time if those Nazis are going to take their uniforms out of mothballs."

The next day I go to Mr. Maandag's vegetable garden. The earth is soft there. I start digging with my hands. Gleaming black beetles scuttle away, fat earthworms are woken from their sleep. I dig a deep hole.

Then I go back home. I bring my toys to the garden in stages. I throw my crayons, roller skates, building blocks, whip and top, all of it, into the hole. Just as I'm dropping in the last pieces of my doll's tea set, Simon appears at the little gate.

"What are you doing?" he asks.

"Nothing," I say gruffly. But he comes closer and leans forward.

"Why are you throwing your toys in there?" He points.

"Don't tell anyone," I whisper, "it's a secret. I'm burying them, because as soon as the SS come they'll take them all away and give them to other children."

"Why do you care?" says Simon, shrugging. "If the SS come, they'll kill you. And if you're dead you won't be able to play anyway."

"Yes, but I don't want Nellie to get my toys." Simon thinks for a moment.

"Maybe they'll give them all to Ineke Bogers," he volunteers soothingly.

"To Ineke?" I say shrilly, pushing sand around. "She's the last person I want to have them! She squashed a June bug with her foot yesterday. And anyway, she stinks!"

When the hole has been filled we stamp on the earth together.

"Swear you won't tell a soul!" I say. Simon nods. "Not even the SS?" He nods again.

Silently we shut the little gate behind us.

Now that my toys are gone, the house seems empty and strange, as if I myself had left as well. I haven't buried Teddy, though. He'll just have to be gassed along with me, even though it isn't healthy. To get him used to the idea, I cuff his ears every now and then.

"*Sauhund!*" I shout as I do it. "Dirty dog!"

The Longest Night

"Suddenly there it was, the rumor. Apparently an inmate of Bergen-Belsen had written a letter describing the place as a holiday camp: you got much more to eat there than in other concentration camps, you didn't have to do hard labor, and the sick were given excellent care.

"It wasn't long before we were talking about nothing else. No one knew who had sent the letter, and none of us had actually seen it, but everyone knew from hearsay that it had been written in ink and on good ruled paper. How it had reached us remained a mystery.

" 'Delivered by a whistling postman, no doubt, cycling from one camp to the next,' said a friend of mine, who didn't believe a word of it either.

"A few days later an official notice from the SS was posted in all the barracks: anyone who felt too weak to work was to apply for a hospital transport to Bergen-Belsen on a date to be announced later. Part of the journey had to be made on foot. Those who did not feel up to this were strongly urged to say so. Special trains were to be arranged for them.

"This happened in the winter of nineteen forty-four, when most of the prisoners could hardly stand. Sick and famished as we were, it was very tempting to believe in the existence of such a letter, and of such a camp, where you would be fed and cared for.

" 'Don't fall for it,' I said to the others. 'It's absolute suicide. All they want is to find out which of us are no longer fit for work. This way they don't even have to go to the trouble of running a selection.'

"And yet, defying all logic, ten men in our barracks did put their names forward. The night before their departure they huddled together by the door, ready to leave at the crack of dawn. The deception was complete. They had been issued new clothes, which, if possible, were even more wretched than their old things, but which had obviously fired their imagination, for they spoke excitedly about the food and medical assistance waiting for them in Bergen-Belsen.

"It was the longest night of my life. I had the runs, and had to scramble down from my bunk three tiers up over and over again to go to the latrine. I kept passing the group of waiting men.

" 'Come on, come with us,' they said, 'then at least we'll be together. We have nothing to lose but one another.'

"Each time I elbowed my way past them, they sang like sirens in my ears, and each time I had to force myself not to join them. As soon as I had climbed back onto my bunk, doubts would begin to gnaw at me.

"Surely, it couldn't be worse in Bergen-Belsen than it was here? Why not take the risk? And if the worst came to the worst, wasn't it better to die among friends than to stay behind on my own? So there I lay, torturing myself, until finally I dozed off.

"The next morning I saw my friends at the edge of the assembly ground. They and the other applicants were standing in rows of five waiting for the transport. Some had wrapped a horse blanket around them, which flapped in the wind. As the roll call got into full swing, I watched them leave out of the corner of my eye: a procession of snow-covered scarecrows who looked in danger of being blown away out of their rags. Perhaps that is what actually happened, for none of them ever returned."

Barter

"Everything we owned, from the rags we wore to our daily portion of watery soup, was the property of the Third Reich. Even our lives were on loan to us from the German state, which could give us notice to quit at any time. The fact that we were allowed to work ourselves to death in the camp instead of being murdered was considered a privilege.

"Anyone who traded in *Reichseigentum*, state property, by bartering food for cigarettes, for instance, or vice versa, was committing a punishable offense. He forfeited all privileges, including his life, generally on the gallows. But anyone who didn't barter was a dead man anyway. You just had to barter. The camp was one big flea market.

Barter

"Soon after I arrived, I became the partner of a Frenchman who worked in the laundry. At night, after roll call, I would rush there like greased lightning and collect the shirt with stand-up collar he would throw out of the window. That sort of shirt was in great demand with the block leaders. I would pick it up, stuff it under my clothes, and go to bargain with it in one of the transit barracks. The number of prisoners there changed all the time, with the result that the block leader was left with extra rations every day. He would pay me in bread, half of which I took to my French partner.

"One day, when handing over a shirt, I was paid with genuine pumpernickel, neatly wrapped in silver paper. As I strolled off with it, I was buttonholed by a Russian, who wanted to buy it from me. He offered me fifteen cigarettes.

" 'Fifteen?' I asked incredulously, because the going price for one bread ration was seven cigarettes. 'That's right,' he said. 'And you can always bring your bread to me.'

"That man was a gold mine. I would buy bread rations at the going rate of seven cigarettes each and trade them with him for fifteen cigarettes each, which meant a clear profit of eight cigarettes every time. I got richer and richer. Pretty soon I was known as the number-one hustler in my block. At night, when I went to the latrine, other prisoners would respectfully make way for me. And while I was sitting there with my pants down around my ankles, they would show up offering me all sorts of goods for sale:

a pair of socks, a leather belt, you name it and they wanted to exchange it for cigarettes. Some even took out an interest-free advance of two cigarettes against the bread ration they would sell me the following night.

"I was trading furiously until my Russian was suddenly gassed. Luckily I discovered that he'd only been an intermediary for another Russian, one Grysha, who belonged to an *Arbeitskommando* making up parcels for German soldiers at the front. He paid twenty cigarettes for one bread ration, five of which his late agent, by way of commission, had pocketed himself.

"For weeks, I did business with Grysha. But his prosperity went to his head. His lordship thought himself too good to work. He bribed his block leader and spent the whole day in his bunk on *Betturlaub,* sick leave. That was bound to end in disaster. One day, the SS came around to inspect and sent him to the gas chamber on permanent leave.

"Nothing in the camp ever lasted. Those who were alive and kicking at morning roll call could be shoveled into the oven an hour later. Without Grysha, I was deprived of my income. Soon afterward I was transferred to an *Aussenlager,* an outside camp, where I was reduced to abject poverty."

Damage

Max is sitting on a chair in front of the refrigerator. The door of the refrigerator is wide open. His socks lie on the kitchen floor.

"What are you doing?" we ask, but he waves us away.

"Leave me alone, I'm doing an experiment."

"You've stuck your bare feet into the refrigerator!" exclaims Simon. Max nods.

"I want to know what it feels like when they freeze."

The light in the refrigerator is on. We peer inside curiously. There lie Max's feet, size eight, on top of the Edam cheese and the sticks of margarine.

"They aren't white yet," says Simon. Max pushes us away.

"They're supposed to go blue, not white!"

"Stop it," says Simon. "Any minute now they'll fall off, and then you won't be able to go roller-skating any more."

Max shrugs.

"Roller-skating is for children."

"What about walking? Is walking for children, too? I thought you wanted to be an explorer!"

"Not any more," answers Max. "I want to be one of them. And you can only be one of them if you're half-starved or if you've had typhus. Being gassed a bit helps, too. Anyway, you have to have suffered damage in some way." He scowls at us. To put him in a good mood, Simon asks how long he's been doing it.

"Seventeen minutes," says Max, looking at his watch, "and they're still not stiff. And if you all keep hanging around, it'll never work!"

He pulls his feet one after the other out of the refrigerator and slams the door shut. The milk bottles clink.

"They haven't fallen off," Simon observes. "They're just wet. Maybe you'll catch pneumonia."

"Pneumonia isn't enough," says Max. "But it's a start. I'd be glad for anything."

"You're crazy!" cries Simon, with tears in his eyes. Max gives him a smack.

"Everybody's crazy in this house!" he says.

"That's not true," Simon sobs. Max laughs.

"And Papa's the craziest of all. What good's a father like that? If Mama had married a farmer, we'd have horses and cows."

He opens the back door and walks barefoot down the gravel path and out of the garden. We watch him go. When he has disappeared from sight, Simon says, "Him and his big mouth! He can't even milk a cow. Can you milk a cow?" I shake my head. "There you are," he says. "Camp is better than cows!"

Animal

"In nineteen forty-four, the factory was bombed," he tells us. "There was a small passageway under the concrete floor, at most three feet wide, where the gas mains ran. You could get into it at the base of the outside wall, through a manhole, which was usually closed with an iron lid. As soon as the first bomb dropped, the SS pulled the cover off and lined us up against the wall. 'Down, you bastards!' It didn't matter to them how we got down: most of us never got a chance to get hold of the narrow ladder, and fell down backwards or head first. But we didn't fall fast enough, so they aimed the fire hoses at us and literally washed us underground.

Animal

"We stood there packed like sardines, soaked to the skin and teeth chattering, the whole time the air raid went on. The earth shook and we rocked backwards and forwards, passageway and all. Because that made the gas pipe behind us creak ominously, we weren't too cheerful either. The SS kept us shut up in there for thirty-six hours. When we were finally allowed up again, the air was so full of smoke we couldn't tell if it was day or night. That could also have been because our eyes had sunk so deep into their sockets with fear that they were somewherre at the back of our heads.

"We walked around in a daze. I fled the smoke and found myself in a part of the factory that was still burning. Suddenly there I was, face to face with Willi Hammer. His sleeve had caught on fire. He was beating the flames out with his cap. How he'd ended up there, I didn't know. What I did know was that he'd never get away from there again.

"As soon as he saw me, he reached into his pants pocket. Scarcely had he brought out the chain with the lead ball than I was sitting on top of him with the chain tight around his neck."

"Did he die?" Max asks. "Did he die?" My father nods.

"I strangled him." He spreads his fingers and looks at them as if they weren't his. "That's something I will never forgive those brutes. They did everything they could to turn me into an animal. A new chapter of the Creation," he laughs grimly. " 'Come, let us make man after our likeness!' And they succeeded. I became their image. I can no longer look in a mirror without coming face to face with a murderer." He bows his head and whispers, "I would do anything to bring Willi back to life, anything! I'd pray for weeks to make that happen. I'd descend to hell to bring him back, even if the road there was paved with splinters of glass and I had to crawl all the way on my belly."

Max goes behind my father's chair and places a hand on his shoulder.

"Then you aren't an animal," he consoles him, "because animals can't feel sorry for what they've done."

"Sorry?" My father curls his upper lip and bares his teeth menacingly. "Sorry? The only reason I want to bring him back to life is so I can murder him all over again. I did it much too quickly the first time. This time I'd take it nice and easy. I'd wring his neck at my leisure, little by little. Now and then I'd give him just enough breath to squirm or scream. The only thing I regret is that I didn't make him suffer in mortal fear long enough."

None of us speaks now. Simon sips his milk but doesn't dare swallow. Now we know why my father keeps strangling his blankets at night. He's practicing for the day when he'll haul Willi back out of hell. He wants to make sure he's still got the right touch.

Popolski

"And just when we thought the worst was over," my father says, "there was the death march. With the Red Army only a few dozen miles away, we were forced to leave the camp."

"Where did you go?" asks Max.

"We left for 'an unknown destination.' There were plans to kill us. Some prisoners were packed into trains that were driven at random all over Europe. Others were loaded onto ships and died when they sank. Some went to camps outside the battle zone. As for us, we had to walk till we dropped."

"But why?" says Max. "What was the point?" My father smiles.

"That very pointlessness fitted in with the Nazis' logic. To the very end the troops remained loyal to their *Führer*. We were driven from village to village with the SS and dogs at our heels. A ludicrous spectacle. Why still bother to shoot at us? We couldn't flee. We were as good as dead already, but they had trained us so well that even our skeletons continued to move at their command."

He lights a cigarette. Another lies smoldering in the ashtray, forgotten.

"The exodus began at the crack of dawn. We watched group after group disappear through the gate. By evening we were still in the camp, looting the deserted barracks. In a *Kapo*'s locker, I discovered a blanket, toothpaste, and thirteen tins of pâté de foie gras from Weisz & Co., Budapest, which I gobbled up on the spot. When we had slept for about an hour, the whistle blew: we had to line up, and then we were marched out in the dark.

"Some four miles outside the camp, we stumbled over the corpses of the people from the hospital block, who had been the first to collapse. We were in pretty bad shape ourselves. I suffered from hunger edema and grew dizzier with every step I took. The blanket over my shoulders weighed a ton. I had to drop it. But I kept the toothpaste. Of all the horrors of that journey, thirst was the worst. Now and then I would squeeze some toothpaste onto my finger and lick it when no one was looking. The stuff burned on my bleeding tongue but it did contain a little moisture.

"We marched for weeks, leaving a trail of corpses. The German version of Tom Thumb. Some days we'd walk for twelve hours, on others for twenty or more at a stretch. Whenever the SS felt like it, it was *'Kolonne halt!'* and we were allowed to rest at the side of the road. During the march we passed other columns sitting on the verge, columns that would later overtake us in their turn. Looking into the eyes of these men was like seeing hundreds of mirrors of your own misery.

"Only the Poles were still fit. As we trudged past them on the grass, they slapped their knees with malicious glee. They shouted insults and spat at us. We'd gladly have ripped out their throats with our teeth, but that was impossible: anyone falling out of line was immediately shot in the back of the neck.

"I've forgotten how long it took before the Poles began to croak. One afternoon we came to a crossroads where they were all lying around dead like flies. Because their bodies were blocking the road, we had to climb over them. Even though I could only lift my feet off the ground with the greatest difficulty, I felt myself grow as light as a feather. I stepped from one Pole onto the next with ease. I would cheerfully have climbed a mountain range at that moment if it had been made of Polish corpses.

"A little further up the road, a group of Poles was sitting at the side of the road, too exhausted to curse. What reserves they had built up in the camp had been spent, and their status had dwindled to that of any prisoner. As soon as we saw them, we bared our teeth like baboons and shook our fists at them.

" 'Hey, Popolski!' we jeered. 'There's a load of your dead bodies over there at the crossroads. They're stinking to high heaven already!' "

My father's mouth is open. His fists are clenched so hard that the blood has drained from them.

"There must have been other kinds of Poles, too, weren't there?" Max asks almost imploringly.

"Maybe so," says my father, "but they were remarkably well hidden because I never met a single one."

"That's horrible!" says Max. "You were more dead than alive and yet you went on hating each other like poison!" My father shuts his eyes.

"Without liberty and equality," he sighs, "it seems fraternity doesn't do too well either."

When Simon and I are brushing our teeth, he slips the toothpaste into the pocket of his pajama jacket.

"We'll take it along to school tomorrow," he whispers.

"What for? We aren't going on a death march, are we?" I say.

"You never know," Simon replies. "Anything might happen."

Shit

"In the end I reached a Russian transit camp close to the American zone. As it turned out, I was further away from home than ever. The Soviets promised to lay on transport for us, but they weren't about to wear themselves out doing it. Why should they, when we were so well off with them, weren't we? In fact, we were so damned well off that most of us came to a bad end as a result.

"Breakfast alone consisted of half a loaf of bread and a couple of pints of greasy pea soup. For lunch and supper we had venison. The Russians machine-gunned the deer by the dozen, and I'd be amazed if there was even half a deer left running around in those woods today.

Shit

"Our guts couldn't handle such mountains of food anymore, of course. Many of the most emaciated prisoners among us stuffed themselves for all they were worth. All around us people lay dying in their own shit.

"We slept in a gigantic barn, and I lay there dozing most of the day as well. I'd put a bale of straw under each of my buttocks with a gap in between through which the shit could pour away. That's how I kept myself more or less clean.

"Weeks went by. Every afternoon American soldiers would show up in the camp, their jeeps crammed with rum, Coca-Cola, and cigarettes. They came to fool around with the Russian Army girls. At night they'd dive into the straw, the pants of their uniforms flying past our ears, and at about three in the morning they would return to their own zone, blind drunk. No wonder they forgot to take us along. The following day another group took a turn at dancing, drinking, and making love, while we lay dying a few yards away.

"Then, one day, a British truck drove onto the site. The Russian girls immediately rushed forward to turn on the gramophone and pour vodka, but the English said, 'Nix vodka! Sign papers!' They picked out ten scarecrows, me included.

"To get to the British transit camp you had to cross the American zone. We all had dysentery and on the way we asked the driver to stop.

" 'Impossible!' said one of the officers sitting with us in the back. 'If you're discovered, the Americans will send you right back to the Russians because according to the regulations it's their job to get you out of there. The fact that they refuse to do so is another matter. The Allies are in this country to get normal life going again, and the Americans have their own sweet way of getting on with it.'

"So we drove non-stop to a large German villa, which the British had set up as their headquarters. We were welcomed with open arms. A couple of lady secretaries served us tea and thickly buttered crackers. No sooner had we got those under our belts than we had to head for the open window and jump out. There on the lawn, smooth as a billiard table, we dropped our pants. Teapot in hand, the girls watched politely while we fouled the grass like dogs."

"Jesus," sighs Max, "I would have died of embarrassment." My father smiles.

"We didn't give a shit. Or rather that's all we had to give."

Bette

"I can't remember where I got it from," says my father, "but I was wearing a German general's overcoat, a gray one with gold epaulets. It came down almost to my ankles. At night I used it as a blanket or rolled it up as a pillow. But mostly I wore it over my concentration camp rags.

"I hadn't had a bath since I was liberated. The Russians would spray clouds of DDT up my sleeves and down the legs of my pants every day, but I was still crawling with lice. The English used DDT, too. I wasn't allowed to have a real bath, no doubt because I hadn't been able to get rid of my fever.

"One day our truck reached a French transit camp.

They ran up to us, all excited. From the distance, they had mistaken me for a German general, but then they saw my gaunt face between the epaulets.

" 'You idiot!' said the commandant. 'Do you think it's funny to go around dressed like that?'

"When I explained that I had no other clothes, he immediately sent a couple of orderlies to the nearest small town with instructions to requisition clothing. And we also got a bathtub. There was a large horse trough in the yard, which captured SS-men had to fill with buckets of water. We climbed in, five of us scarecrows at a time.

"That afternoon several trucks showed up with Frenchmen who had been doing forced labor service in Germany. They were spilling out of the backs of the trucks, bawling socialist songs and waving the French flag. As soon as we caught sight of them, we scrambled out of the trough and began waving back at them, stark naked. They threw the back flaps open, leaped out, and danced with us around the trucks, singing the 'Marseillaise.' "

Still talking, my father gets up from his chair. He stretches out his arms and takes strange skipping steps through the room. *"Allons enfants de la patrie,"* he sings, *"le jour de gloire est arrivé!"* It looks more like a Russian dance than a French one. We sit there, subdued. When he has finished, he goes behind my mother's chair, leans over her, and kisses her on the mouth.

"And what happened then?" we ask.

Bette

"That night the orderlies came back with clothes for us. I got an old-fashioned black worsted tailcoat with impressive braiding. It had once belonged to some Reichstag deputy, a dwarf, if you ask me, because the sleeves came to just past my elbows and the tails ended at my waist. The pants weren't much better either. I looked as if I'd escaped from a circus. I came back home in those clothes, weeks later, to Bette."

He bends over my mother.

"Remember?" he says. "You flung your arms around my neck in the street, but I was so weak that I fell over backwards onto the cobblestones." He laughs. "And you lay on top of me and just kept on moaning, 'What have they done to you, Ephraim, what have they done to you?' "

Tears run from my mother's dark eyes. We look at her face, shocked. We are seeing it today for the first time. It is the face of Papa's sweetheart. Her name is Bette, and she waited for him.

"I remember everything," she says calmly, as her cheeks become shining wet. "Everything."

A Note About the Author

Carl Friedman was born in 1952 in Eindhoven, the Netherlands. She lived for many years in Antwerp, Belgium, then returned to the Netherlands in 1977. Originally a translator, journalist, and poet whose work was published in major Dutch literary periodicals, Friedman published *Tralievader*, her first novel, in 1991. *Nightfather* is the English version of this novel. It has also been translated into German. Her second novel, *Twee koffers vol*, was published in the Netherlands in 1993 and will be published in English in the United States in 1995. Carl Friedman now lives in Amsterdam with her son, and is working on her third book.